Zonk

the dreaming tortoise

By
David Hoobler

Dedicated to Ilene and my mom, Florene.

A special thanks to my sister Rennie Kirby.

Zonk Galleries
P.O. Box 11059
Oakland, CA 94611
510-530-2681

www.zonktheturtle.com

The illustrations for this book are rendered in watercolor and ink.

First edition, third printing.
Printed in Singapore.

Summary: A tortoise in the Sonoran Desert decides he'd like to find the ocean and become a sea turtle.

ISBN 0-9706537-0-0

Zonk

the dreaming tortoise

by David Hoobler

This is a map of the Sonoran Desert where Zonk lives with his family and friends. The Sonoran Desert is often very hot and there is little water.

For Mateo,
Be a dreamer!

Dave Hoobler

6/2/13

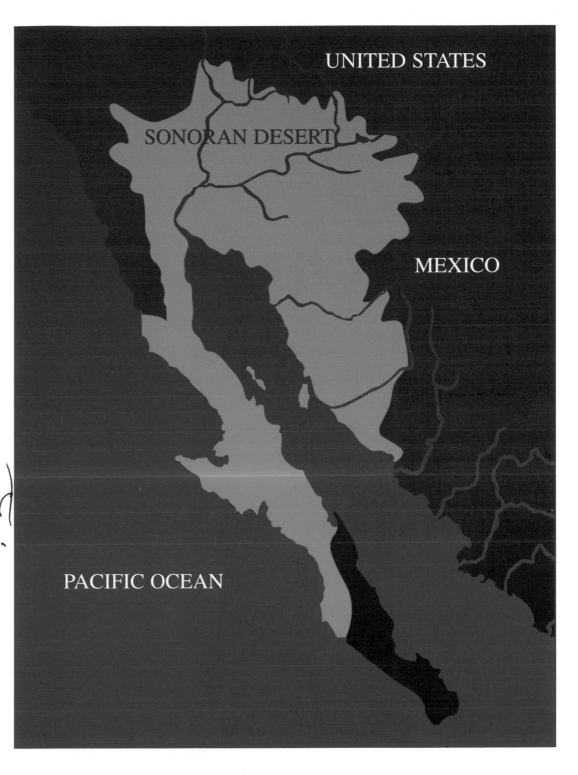

UNITED STATES

SONORAN DESERT

MEXICO

PACIFIC OCEAN

"Look! A flying turtle!"
Zonk shouted. Zonk and his friends Bunny, Snake and Coyote were exploring and had found a rock with pictures painted on it.

"It's a sea turtle, and he's swimming not flying," said Coyote, who knew everything.

"What's swimming?" asked Zonk.

"See that bird flying through the air?" said Coyote. "Swimming is like flying in water. Sea turtles live in the ocean and there's water everywhere."

Water everywhere! Everyone laughed. What an idea!

All the way home
Zonk daydreamed of
the sea turtle and
swimming.

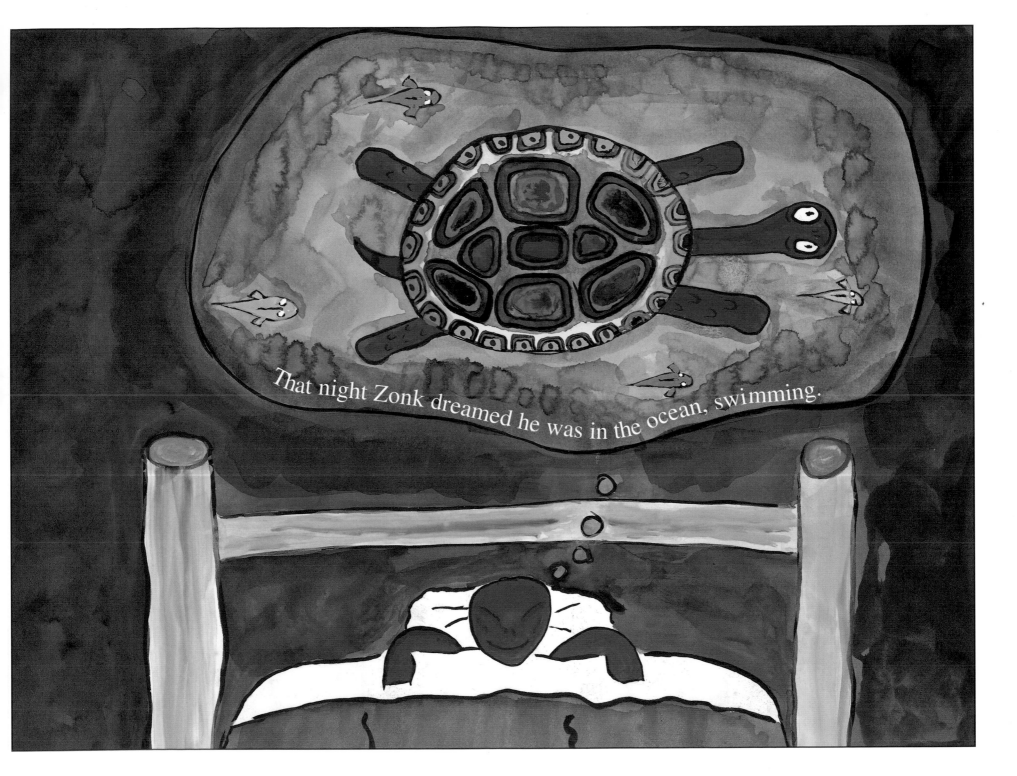

That night Zonk dreamed he was in the ocean, swimming.

Wow!" Zonk shouted as he splashed through the waves. In the water he felt light as a feather, like a bird. Then, along came Fish.

"What are you doing here?"

"What's it look like? Swimming of course," Zonk replied.

"I happen to know a sea turtle can swim and a desert tortoise cannot," Fish pointed out.

"Well I can swim," said Zonk.

"You're dreaming," Fish said and swam away.

Zonk woke up.

Zonk asked his Mom and Dad where the ocean was. "I'm going to learn to swim like a sea turtle"

"I've never seen the ocean," said Zonk's mom.

"Water everywhere, who ever heard of such a thing," Zonk's dad scoffed. "Silly Zonk!"

Zonk asked his friends Bunny, Snake and Coyote to help him.

"It's probably cold and you won't find any prickly pear cactus to eat," said Snake. "Silly Zonk!"

"Why are you looking for the ocean, Zonk?" Asked Bunny. "It's too far. Besides what would you eat? Saguaro fruit doesn't grow in the ocean. Silly Zonk!"

Coyote shifted
his ears and growled.
"G-r-r-r. The ocean is a
bad place for a tortoise.
You could drown.
Silly Zonk!"

Coyote had a point. Zonk decided he had better learn to swim. Zonk went out into the desert where he thought he was all alone. He balanced himself on top of a dune and started practicing swimming. He imagined himself floating on a cool quiet ocean.

Behind the barrel cactus his friends Bunny, Coyote and Snake watched and laughed.

"HEE, HEE, HEE! Look at Silly Zonk!"

Feeling embarrassed Zonk went to hide.

Zonk climbed the highest bluff hoping he would see the ocean, but all he saw was a Saguaro covered in his favorite fruit.

Deep in the canyon stood the skeleton of the oldest cactus, the Spirit of the Saguaro. Her flesh and thorns were gone, only her bleached bones rattled in the wind.

Shaking from head to toe and with Bunny, Snake and Coyote following behind, Zonk tiptoed carefully to the Spirit of the Saguaro to ask his question.

"Ancient Spirit of the Saguaro, can you tell us where the ocean is?" Silence roared up and down the gorge!

Coyote whispered, "Spanish, ask in Spanish!"

"Donde esta el oceano?" Zonk asked The Spirit.

The Spirit answered.
"No mas sabemos lo que sabemos!"

We only know what we know? What
does it mean?" Zonk felt hopeless.

"I don't know, it's all she ever says,"
answered Coyote. As Zonk and his
friends headed home The Spirit
went to work. She spoke to the
wind that whistled through her bones.

High up over the mountains the wind whispered The Spirit's message. The hot air and cold air began fighting a terrible fight. Lightning, fierce wind and bellows of thunder rolled over the desert.

The hot air and cold air became tired and fell from the sky on to the mountain. They turned into rain as they fell. This was the monsoon, the hot summer rain.

Zonk had given up trying to find the ocean. He was down in the wash munching away at some beavertail cactus.

The monsoon moved out over the desert, turning the dry washes into creeks and rivers. The creeks and rivers became a racing flash flood heading for Zonk.

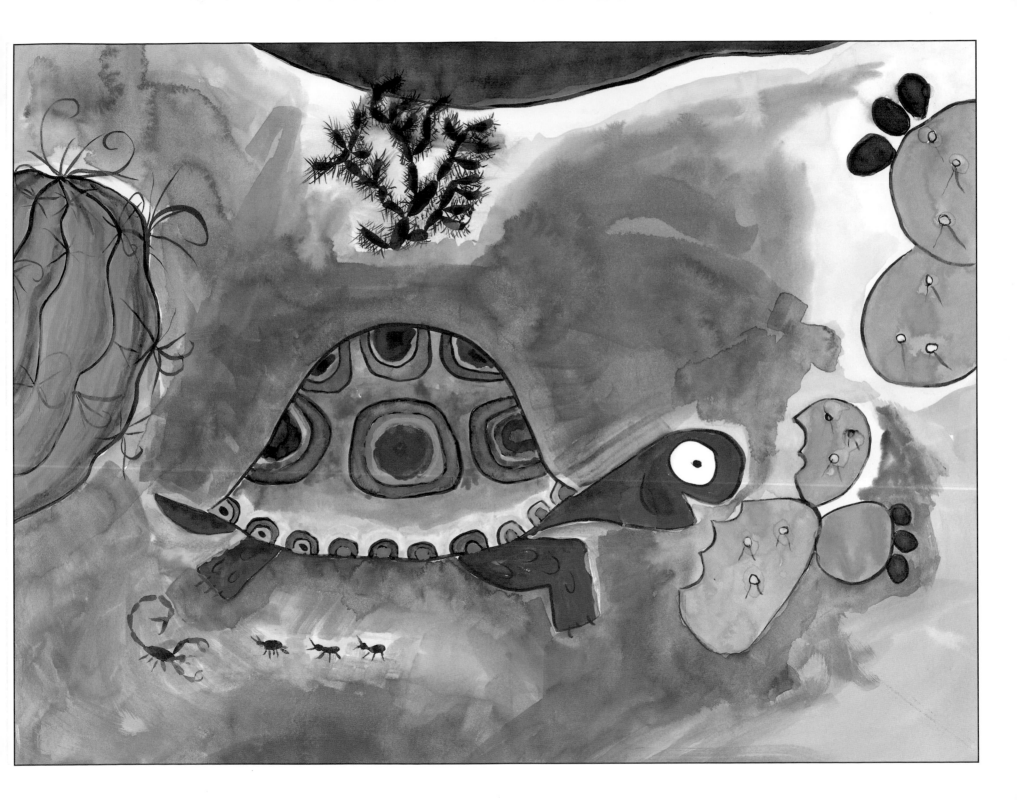

zonk went

tumbling

tumbling

tumbling

The water slowed, became peaceful and deeper.

"I'm in the ocean! It's my dream come true."

Then he sank like a rock.
Zonk panicked,
"What can I do!"

Zonk remembered Coyote's words, "flying in water". He remembered his swimming practice in the dunes. He started kicking his legs. Slowly he began moving through the water. Coyote was right, swimming was like flying in water. Zonk burst to the surface and shouted, "Air!"

Zonk paddled and the waves lifted him up and down. Suddenly Fish jumped out of the water and over Zonk's head. He scared Zonk and disappeared into the waves. "Oh no," thought Zonk, "It's Fish, trying to spoil my dream come true."

Fish reappeared and asked, "Who are you?"

Zonk looked him right in the eye and said, "I'm Zonk the Sea Tortoise."

Jumping out of the water into the sunlight Fish shouted back, "Hi Zonk! Happy to meet you."

Zonk paddled away with his new friends to find new adventures in the ocean.